Max Velthuijs
Elephant and Crocodile

Translated by Anthea Bell

Farrar, Straus and Giroux
New York

Crocodile was a musician. He played the violin, and he practiced all day, every day, until late into the night. It gave him great satisfaction.

However, it was no fun for his neighbor. Hearing the same tune over and over again, with wrong notes, too, got on Elephant's nerves.

One day he could bear it no longer. He went over to
Crocodile's place to complain.

But Crocodile said he was an artist. "I can't live without my music!" he told Elephant.

Elephant went home feeling depressed.

That evening, Crocodile played his violin again. As usual, he played until late into the night.

And so it went.
Crocodile played his violin, out of tune, and it got on
Elephant's nerves.
Elephant couldn't read anymore. He couldn't sleep either.

In fact, all the pleasure had gone out of Elephant's life, and he
went to the doctor about his poor nerves.
The doctor prescribed peace and quiet and some nasty medicine.
But once Elephant was home, Crocodile's wrong notes got on
his nerves worse than ever.
How nice to be an artist like Crocodile, he thought.

And then, all of a sudden, Elephant thought, well, why not? Who knows, maybe I'm an artist, too!
He went to town, all excited, and bought himself a beautiful, shiny brass trumpet.
He had wanted a trumpet like it ever since he was little.

That evening he began to practice.
Oh, what fun it was!
Elephant was quite surprised by his own musical gifts.
He played and played until late into the night.

Crocodile, who had just been learning a violin sonata by
Mozart, was very surprised when he suddenly heard a terrible
noise next door.
"What's going on?" he shouted angrily.
Elephant must be off his rocker, he thought.
He went over to Elephant's place at once.

"Stop that noise!" said Crocodile furiously. "You're ruining my music!"
But Elephant didn't get ruffled.
"My dear Crocodile," he said. "I'm sorry, but you see, I'm an artist, too. I can't live without my trumpet."

Poor Crocodile. He couldn't play music anymore. Elephant's trumpet was too loud.
Crocodile could hardly hear his own violin.

Elephant, on the other hand, was fine.
Discovering his musical talent had changed him completely.
He let his hair grow and wore the sort of clothes that
everybody noticed.
He was as happy as the day is long, and had more fun than ever
blowing his shiny brass trumpet.

Crocodile did his best to drown out Elephant's noise with saucepan lids.

Which meant that Elephant had to blow louder than ever.
And so the two neighbors went on annoying each other.

In desperation, Crocodile started using his pneumatic drill.

The noise was too much for Elephant! He collapsed on the floor in a fright.

This time Crocodile had gone too far.

Elephant took his sledgehammer and hit the wall as hard as he could. Again and again.

The wall couldn't stand up to that. It fell down with a loud crash.
There stood the two artists face to face, looking very surprised.

"I didn't mean that to happen," stammered Elephant. "Can I offer you a cup of tea?"

So the neighbors had tea and discussed their love of music.
"I know!" said Elephant. "Why don't we play together?"
"What a good idea!" said Crocodile.
He went straight off to fetch his violin, which was underneath
the rubble.

Then the two of them played music together, in perfect time –
one, two, three, four!
They played for hours. They played for weeks. They got better
and better. It was lovely!

They became famous all over the world for their duets, and they lived happily together ever after.
They never rebuilt the wall.
They didn't need it now.